For Mark, James, Joe and Jess ~

JH

For Fay and Peter Babenko ~

MM

First published in 2009 by Scholastic Children's Books
Euston House, 24 Eversholt Street
London NW1 1DB
a division of Scholastic Ltd
www.scholastic.co.uk
London ~ New York ~ Toronto ~ Sydney ~ Auckland
Mexico City ~ New Delhi ~ Hong Kong

HB ISBN: 978 1407 10553 6
PB ISBN: 978 1407 10554 3

Wishmole

and the Little Piece of Sky

Written by
Julia Hubery

Illustrated by
Mary McQuillan

SCHOLASTIC

Down in the dark, delicious
earth, most moles are happy,
dig-dig-digging.

But Wishmoley wanted more:
he wished to see the world above.

"Above is too big and bright for a little mole," said his mummy. "Look at your spadey paws, and your lovely, shovelly nose! Moles are made for digging. Moles are made for Under."

Wishmoley tried to be a good, happy
digger, but he couldn't help wondering
if Above was better than Under.
So one day he tunnelled up, up, up. . .

. . . and popped
his head Above.

He looked at the busy, bustling world.
It was all so strange and new.

He felt afraid.

But then he looked up at the sky.
It was calm and blue.
It was beautiful.
He wished he could have
his own little piece of sky.

Then, from way up high, something fell:
something smooth and round and
warm, and as blue as the sky.

"Thank you!"
whispered Wishmoley.

Then he carefully picked
up his piece of sky,
and carried it Under.

"Look, Mummy! It's from Above,"
he said. "I wished for some of the
beautiful blue, and down it came!"

Wishmoley treasured
his piece of sky, and took
it with him everywhere.

One morning, the little piece
of sky began to quiver.

A *tap-tap-tapping* came

from inside, louder and louder.

Suddenly it broke apart . . .

. . . and a tiny, ugly thing crept out!
It snuggled next to Wishmoley, cheeping.

"What is it?" he cried.

"It's a baby," said Mummy, "and
it needs to be loved."

Wishmoley soon had
lots of digging to do.
His baby needed worms
and grubs, so he dug
and dug to find them.

Then she grew too big for
her little nest, so he had
to dig another one.
And still Baby grew,
so he dug another . . .

and another!

Wishmoley was happy digging,
because Baby loved him,
and he loved Baby. She
sang while he worked,
and she tried to help.

But Baby wasn't made for digging:
she had the wrong kind of paws,
and she couldn't shovel at all.
She cheeped sadly.

"Baby is crying!" Wishmoley
told Mummy. Wishmoley
wished he could make
Baby happy again.

Mummy hugged him tightly.
"You have to be brave to make her happy,"
she said, "for Baby is a bird, and she
doesn't belong Under.
She belongs Above."

So Wishmoley dug up, up, up . . .
Above. Baby flapped the dirt
off of her wings, and hopped
and fluttered happily.

She flapped and hopped and fluttered, until . . .

Baby flew!

As Wishmoley watched her
he felt proud, and sad.

"Why are you sad?" Baby asked.

"Because some day you'll fly higher than high, and the blue will fill your eyes, and maybe you'll forget to come down," said Wishmoley.

Baby snuggled next to him. "I'll never forget," she said.

One bright morning, a bird just like Baby
swooped through the sky, and Baby
flew up to say hello. Wishmoley watched . . .
and he knew he had to be very brave.

When she flew down he kissed her.
  "You're not a baby any more," he said.
"It's time to fly with the other birds,
where you belong."

"But you'll be sad," cried Baby.
"Oh no," said Wishmoley, "I'll be
happy dig-dig-digging, and thinking
of you, up in the blue."

Baby hugged Wishmoley, then
up she flew, up and away.

Most moles are happiest, dig-dig-digging.
But sometimes a little mole comes up Above,
and listens as a song falls from the sky . . .

and he smiles.